Bump in
the Night

Ruth Morgan

Illustrated by
Chris Glynn

First Impression—2001

ISBN 1 85902 944 2

© text: Ruth Morgan
© illustrations: Chris Glynn

2458992 6

This volume is published with the support of the
Arts Council of Wales.

Printed in Wales at
Gomer Press, Llandysul, Ceredigion SA44 4QL

For the children of
Peter Lea Primary School

Chapter 1

The Call

Unfortunately, Uncle Wil 'phoned just as Mam and I were in the middle of another row about that rotten bridesmaid's dress.

'I don't care what you say,' (she was starting to turn purple at this point), 'it's our Avril's big day next Saturday and you are turning up in that lovely dress, like it or not!'

Brring, brring . . .

'I look like a frilly pink blob in it!' I wailed. 'It doesn't fit and it looks awful.'

'That's why it's gone back to the dress shop to be altered. I've explained this about a hundred times.'

'I won't smile for the photos.' I'd made that threat about a hundred times, too.

Brring, brring . . .

Mam walked to the 'phone as calmly as she could and lifted the receiver. Her face fell when she heard the familiar voice.

'It's Uncle Wil, for you,' she sighed. 'That's all we need – my batty brother sticking his oar in.'

I'd been expecting him to call and pounced excitedly on the receiver but Mum snatched it away at the last moment.

'Ah, no you don't – not until you promise to wear that dress,' she said.

'Aw Mam, this is really important!'

'And so is this.'

Uncle Wil used to work at Barry Island until he hurt his back and he misses the fairground a lot. Now if the fairground owner wants to get rid of anything, he gives Wil a call. And when Wil gets a call, I get a call.

'They've come, Lauren *bach*! I've got them right here in the yard – two of them,'

He sounded puffed out with excitement.

'I'll be there now, in a minute.'

Crashing the 'phone down, I sped out to the shed to get my bike. Mam said, yes, I could go over to Wil's, I could even spend the night (I did that sometimes), just as long as I was back at ten in the morning to go to the dress shop for another fitting. I had to agree or she wouldn't have let me go.

Cycling up the hill on my way to Wil's, I was half excited at what he'd have to show me but still half furious at the thought of having to wear the hideous pink blob again.

Chapter 2

Uncle Wil

It's a good job Mam hasn't visited Wil lately. She'd get the shock of her life.

You go in through the front door and come face to face with a hundred different reflections of yourself. Your body might suddenly be enormous while your head has shrunk to the size of a pea, or your legs and arms have become so thin and ribbony, if you jump up and down you look like a jellyfish with hiccups at a disco. Uncle Wil's hall is a real hall of mirrors!

And because there are mirrors on both sides, you see yourself reflected again and again and again. 'To infinity,' Wil says.

Slowly, Wil is turning his house into a fairground, or the closest he can get to it. He had his stairs taken away and a helter skelter put in, (handy if you're running a bit late in the morning). He sleeps in a swingboat and keeps his clothes in an old coffin from the Haunted House of Horror.

This particular day, I knew he'd got his hands on something special, something he'd been after for a very long time.

Wil was standing on the doorstep as I arrived, waving his arms wildly.

'They're here, they're here!' he yelled. 'Come on – what took you so long?'

He grabbed my arm, barely giving me time to chain my bike to the railings, and yanked me inside.

'They're in pretty poor condition,' he panted, 'but that's no problem. I've some fairground paint in the shed. We can give them a lick of it this afternoon.'

He whisked me through the kitchen (past his hot dog stand) and out into the yard.

'Wow – they're great!' I gasped.

There, side by side, sat two bumper cars – one red and one blue, although they were pretty bashed about and rusty.

'What are you going to do with them, though?'

Wil removed his flat cap and scratched his bald head.

'Dunno yet,' he frowned. 'A couple of armchairs, maybe? It does seem a shame just to have them sit there, though. Not see them move about, like.'

I jumped into the red one and gripped the small steering wheel in my hands. Of course, nothing happened as I turned the wheel – how could it? – but as I shut my eyes there I was at the fairground, with the noise and the lights and the rushing wind as my little car hurtled around aiming for something to bump.

'Wow, great,' I muttered, gritting my teeth. It crossed my mind that there *was* something I wouldn't mind hitting with this little bumper car, something pink and flouncy that I'd like to hit off its hanger and grind into the mud.

I opened my eyes. Wil was still scratching his head.

'Nope. They won't want to be armchairs,' I said.

Chapter 3

Bump in the Night

We spent all afternoon painting the cars. Wil took the blue one and I took the red. Every so often, I couldn't resist climbing in and there it was before my eyes again – the dreaded pink blob in its full horror. I imagined it squelching under the wheels of the car and hearing that wonderful ripping sound. There'd be no time to make another before the wedding and I'd be able to go along in my black mini dress.

As a finishing touch, we painted faces on the front of each car. Then over hot dogs, Wil and I discussed our handiwork.

'Superb,' Wil said. 'We've done a grand job. Now I think we should give them names. Mine's going to be called Blue Bertie.'

'And mine's going to be called . . .' I stopped. What would be a suitable name for my car?

'Hmm, don't you think you've made him look rather angry?' Wil said.

It was true. Wil's car sported an angelic little smile whereas mine looked as if it were snarling at something.

'I'll just have to call him the Red Devil,' I said.

It was gone midnight when I was woken by the noise coming from the yard. I could see the alarm clock on the little table next to my swingboat bed. The noise was a steady bump . . . bump . . . bump . . . not very loud, just as though the wind were rattling the wooden gates.

I listened hard. If it was the wind, how come it wasn't blowing the branches of next door's tree? And Wil's house was so old, you could always hear a wind whistling down the chimney.

Bump . . . bump . . . bump . . . Was it getting louder or was it just my imagination? I jumped out of bed and went to the window overlooking the yard.

It was so dark, I could hardly see a thing but now I was certain the noise was getting louder.

Bump . . . bump . . . bump . . .

As my eyes grew used to the dark, I saw it!

I ran next door to Wil's room, yelling, 'Wil, get up!'

'Wh . . . what is it, girl?' he yelled back, fumbling for the bedside light.

'I – I think . . . You're not going to believe this but . . .'

'What is it? What's that noise?'

The bumping stopped, only to be followed by an enormous CRACK, a CRUNCH and what sounded like a shower of splinters hitting the ground.

We whizzed down to the hallway and ran to the back door. Wil grabbed a torch and shone its beam out into the yard.

'What the . . !' Wil gasped.

'Oh no!' I gulped.

'What's all the racket about?' Mrs Evans next door had her head stuck out of an upstairs window and there were lights going on in other houses, too.

'Erm – sorry about that, nothing to worry about, it's all over now,' Wil said in a commanding tone.

Mrs Evans moaned a bit then went back to bed.

One by one the other lights went out as well. At least no one else had seen what we had seen. What we were *still* staring at now.

The yard was covered in splinters of wood. Poor little Bertie was cowering in the corner while there in the back gate was a hole the exact size and shape of my own Red Devil . . .

Chapter 4

Follow that Car

There was no time to stand there wondering very long.

'Someone must have stolen the Red Devil!' said Wil. 'Come on – we must go after them.'

He ran inside and grabbed a couple of old coats hanging up by the back door.

'Stick this on,' he said tossing me a red one. 'They can't have gone far.'

We both noticed that Bertie had crept out of his corner with a helpful look on his face. Like I said, there was no time to stand there wondering . . .

We jumped in. Wil gripped the steering wheel and we were off!

It was dark in the back lane. Bertie turned one way, then the other, unsure of which direction to take.

There was rubbish strewn all over the ground as dustbins lay rolling from side to side.

'Hush,' whispered Wil.

All three of us sat and listened.

In the distance came a bump and crash, bump and crash.

'It's coming from over there,' I pointed.

'They must be in the back lanes still,' Wil agreed. 'Come on – let's try and creep up on them.'

Bertie crept along, stopping at every turn, listening to decide which direction to take next.

'This way, bear right . . .'

'No, it's coming from over there!' We argued as we went along but slowly, we did seem to be gaining on them. The bumps and crashes were getting louder and there was rubbish everywhere.

Finally, we could tell the car was just round the next corner, knocking over dustbins.

'Great,' whispered Wil. 'It's a dead end. Are you ready for this, Bertie? We'll jump out and surprise them – the rotten little thieves!'

Bertie revved up (how was he able to do that?)
and we sprang round the corner.

The Red Devil was at full tilt, hurtling down the lane, sending the dustbins flying.

Wil was right: the lane was a dead end. When the car got to the very end, it turned and faced us.

Bertie edged forward. The Red Devil began to snort.

Wil shone his torch. 'Now we've got you, you blinkin' thugs,' he yelled.

We stopped, amazed.

There was no one in the car. Steam was starting to rise from its bonnet and as we watched, its face gave an even more evil sneer.

'Now – er – you're coming back with us,' Wil said firmly. 'Don't try any funny business . . .'

The Red Devil started pawing the ground with his wheels.

Bertie was trembling.

'Let's get out of the way!' I yelled.

It was too late. The Red Devil leapt at us and . . .

BUMP!

Wil and I were thrown from the little blue car. Luckily, we had a soft landing on a pile of bin bags but poor Bertie . . .

Staggering to our feet, we ran over to him. He was lying upside down with a huge dent in his side from where he'd fallen.

And as we heaved Bertie over onto his wheels again, sinister 'Hee! hee!' sounds echoed in the alleyway. The Red Devil had escaped!

Chapter 5

Down Town

'Wil, I think this might be my fault,' I whispered nervously.

'Your fault? What do you mean?'

Once we'd dusted Bertie down and had given his wheels a tinker, we started off slowly. He gave a few nervous judders, but after that he seemed quite his old self again.

'I was feeling so angry this afternoon, when I was painting the car,' I began. 'Some of what I was feeling must have rubbed off on it. Does that sound daft?'

'Yes, but I'd believe anything tonight,' Wil sighed. 'Which way do you think it went?'

We had come to the end of our part of town. To the left was the sea, while the right took you into the town centre.

Suddenly a terrible thought struck me.

'Wil, don't ask me why, but I think we'd better head for town.'

Bertie seemed to agree as he nudged forward in that direction.

'Righto, full speed ahead!' said Wil.

We were right. It didn't take long before we came to a dented lamp-post followed by an upturned litter bin and the remains of a bed of pansies.

'Hope they don't think I'm paying for this damage,' Wil moaned.

'At least we can see where he's been.'

But I had a sick feeling in my stomach as, moment by moment, I became convinced that I knew where the Red Devil was headed.

'I know where it's going,' I said in a small, guilty voice.

Bertie ground to a halt.

'Well, tell us, then.' Wil spluttered.

'You won't be angry?'

'Just tell us!'

There was no time to lose. Once I'd told Wil and Bertie everything, we sped off towards the High Street.

'Your Mam will never let you see me again,' muttered Wil.

'I know,' I said. 'Just pray we get there in time.'

We got there. It was too late. The window of the dress shop was smashed with a whole pile of silk, tyre-marked wedding dresses on the floor inside. The shop alarm was shrieking, too.

'Let's go or they'll think it was us,' Wil yelled.

We zoomed off up the High Street and we hadn't gone very far before the Red Devil came into view. It was some distance ahead but quite easy to spot on account of a puffy pink sail hooked to the back of it.

'My bridesmaid's dress!' I yelped. 'We've got to get it back or Mam will kill me!'

It was true. How could anyone explain how that was the only dress stolen from the shop?

'Don't panic,' said Wil. 'Now just think. What did you imagine happening to the dress, when you were painting the car this afternoon?'

'I just wanted to grind it into the mud,' I confessed. 'Drive over it and over it until it was ripped to shreds.'

'Mud. Hmm.' Wil was thinking. 'Where would you be most likely to find mud around here?'

'The football pitch!' I shrieked. 'That's where he's going. Come on, Bertie, we've got to try and stop him.'

Chapter 6

A Game of Two Halves

Barry Town football pitch could get extremely muddy at this time of year. As a match had been played that afternoon, it was muddier still.

Wil shone his torch. We could see the Red Devil on the pitch, wheeling about in a figure eight. At least the bridesmaid's dress was still safe, billowing like a balloon, but for how much longer?

'It's now or never,' said Wil.

Bertie revved up and we zoomed onto the pitch.

The Red Devil stopped when he saw us and gave a horrid sneer.

'Stop!' I shouted 'You don't have to do this. I want to wear the dress, I really do.'

For a moment it almost looked as if it understood. Slowing to a standstill, it looked almost apologetic.

'See, it's a nice dress,' I said.

The car actually smiled and nodded.

'So be a good – er – Devil and give it back.'

VVRROOOM!

With an evil laugh, it swung round, splattering us with mud and shot off up the pitch.

'After him,' Wil yelled. The chase was on.

We chased after the Red Devil for a good twenty mintues. It started tossing the dress high in the air, catching it just in the nick of time. After a while, Bertie ground to a halt, panting.

'He's playing with us,' I said. 'We've got to distract him in some way.'

'. . . And I think I know how,' Wil replied. 'Take your coat off. I've only seen this done on telly but it seems to work with bulls.'

I took off the red coat and passed it to Wil, who stood up in his seat and started flapping it in the air.

'*Toro! Toro!*' he called.

The Red Devil turned round and spotted the coat. Lowering his head and pawing the muddy ground with his wheels, he suddenly charged towards us.

'*Ole!*' cried Wil, snatching the coat away at the last minute. The Red Devil passed underneath and out the other side.

Bertie swung round and Wil repeated the performance with great shouts of '*Toro*' and '*Ole,*' just like a real bullfighter.

Soon, the Red Devil was really losing its temper. Its nostrils flared and its teeth clashed in anger.

We'd got it over as far as the goalposts.

'One last time!' cried Wil.

The car passed under the coat into the back of the net. Then, finding it couldn't go any further, it started twisting and turning and getting more and more caught up in the net.

'Out of the way, Bertie!' Wil shouted.

We backed away in time to see the whole goalpost crashing down around the Red Devil. It was trapped.

'We'd better rescue that blinkin' dress, then,' said Wil.

Chapter 7

Back to normal?

There are some things in life you'll never be able to explain to the people who weren't there. Perhaps it's better not to.

'Mum, a bumper car stole my bridesmaid's dress from the shop then went beserk with it on the football pitch last night.' Somehow, no.

So what we did was cover our tracks as best we could.

The dress was quite mud-splattered but still in one piece, so we crept back to the shop where the police had been and gone and left it sticking obviously out of a nearby bin.

As for the Red Devil, it took a good couple of hours but we managed to drag it home through the darkened back lanes, still trapped in the net.

Back in the yard, Wil removed its wheels straight away and locked it in the shed.

The papers were full of it for a few days: 'VANDALS ON THE RAMPAGE' but the police couldn't find many leads. Soon, everybody came to the conclusion that the gang of hooligans had passed through town and gone on their way.

Avril's wedding was a happy day all round. My dress looked almost as good as new once it was back from the cleaner's and I smiled for the photos. I did everything I had to because that way, I knew Mam would let me spend the following Saturday at Wil's. On Saturday morning there was to be a grand unveiling ceremony . . .

GRAND
UNVEILING
CEREMONY
SATURDAY 10.30am

Chapter 8

'My Batty Brother'

A huge sheet covered Wil's house. It was loads of sheets sewn together, in fact. People were very interested in what was going on and gangs of kids had been hanging about on the pavement for days. A sign hanging over the roof guttering, said:

GRAND UNVEILING CEREMONY
SATURDAY 10.30 a.m.

I knew all about it but I wasn't letting on, of course. In an effort to please my Mam, Wil had asked her to come along and do the actual unveiling and although she didn't know what on earth it was all about, amazingly she agreed.

Wil had wasted no time in getting to grips with the Red Devil. It was given a new lick of yellow paint and a fresh face, which worked wonders. 'Golden Gertie' was an excellent partner for Blue Bertie and they seemed to take to each other straight away.

The next problem was what to *do* with the cars. A pair of armchairs was right out of the question. Then Wil, as usual, hit on the perfect solution.

The crowds started gathering at ten o'clock. Soon, hundreds of people were waiting, blocking the entire road. Mam arrived at twenty-five-past ten in her best suit. Clearly amazed at the number of people gathered, she teetered down the path and Wil gave her the cord she was to pull.

Wil called for quiet.

'I'd like to say a few words,' he began. 'Lots of you have been wondering what I've been up to and this morning you're going to find out. My dear sister,' (Mam smiled awkwardly) 'has agreed to do the honours and reveal all. All I want to say is you are all welcome at my home: I'm going to open it to the public, although you won't all be able to come at once, of course. All I want is for everyone to enjoy themselves!'

He gave Mam the signal and she pulled the cord. The sheet fell away and the crowd gasped.

A track ran right round the house and over the roof. Wil pulled a lever and the two cars, Bertie and Gertie, appeared on top of the roof and went hurtling down the track, down into the garden pond with a splash.

Then they reappeared, trundled round the corner of the house and in a minute did the same thing again. The crowd went wild! Mam's jaw nearly hit the floor.

'There's more inside for you to see,' Wil shouted. 'My niece Lauren is going to hand out numbered tickets so you'll all have a chance to visit Wil's Wacky Fun House!'

Mam remained speechless. She took a bit of winning over but by the end of the afternoon, she too was persuaded to have a go on Bertie.

'He's nuts,' she said to me after the crowds had gone. 'Completely batty. I don't know where he gets it from. None of the rest of us are like that.' Then she looked at me strangely.

'Oh, Wil's alright,' I said. 'Don't worry. I'll keep an eye on him, make sure he doesn't go too far.'

Then we went in for hot dogs and candy floss.

About the author . . .

I started writing when I was at primary school
in Llandovery. I wrote a secret class newspaper
which eventually got me into hot water . . .
Now I'm a teacher in Cardiff, I still try to find as
much time to write as possible. Writing your own
stories is brilliant because you can have whatever
you like happen. Fantastic!
Bump in the Night, like all my stories, is about
extraordinary happenings in ordinary lives. I hope
you enjoy it.